Daddy, will you miss me?

Wendy McCormick

Illustrated by Jennifer Eachus

ALADDIN PAPERBACKS

New York London Toronto Sydney Singapore

For Ian and Scott
W.R.M.

For Lloyd Phillips
J.E.

First Aladdin Paperbacks edition May 2002

Text copyright © 1999 by Wendy McCormick
Illustrations copyright © 1999 by Jennifer Eachus
Aladdin Paperbacks
An imprint of Simon & Schuster
Children's Publishing Division
1230 Avenue of the Americas
New York, NY 10020
Also available in a Simon & Schuster Books for Young Readers hardcover edition.

Designed by Martin Aggett
The text of this book was set in Perpetua.
The illustrations were done in pencil crayon.
Printed in Belgium.
2 4 6 8 10 9 7 5 3 1

The Library of Congress has cataloged the hardcover edition as follows:
McCormick, Wendy.
Daddy will you miss me? / Wendy McCormick.
Illustrated by: Jennifer Eachus.
p. cm.
Summary: A boy and his daddy come up with lots of different ways
to stay close to one another while the daddy is in Africa for four weeks.
ISBN 0-689-81898-X (hc.)
[1. Fathers and sons—Fiction. 2. Africa—Fiction.] I. Eachus, Jennifer. ill. II. Title.
PZ7.M13695Da] 1999 [E]—dc21 97-45012 AC
ISBN 0-689-85063-8 (Aladdin pbk.)

My daddy's going to work,
far away in Africa—
without me.

"I'll be back," he says.
"Four short weeks isn't that long."
"That's long enough," I say.
"Too long for me."

I sit on his bed while we pack his shirts and shoes
and shaving things.

"What shall I bring you back from Africa?"
my daddy asks me.
"Nothing," I answer, winding his blue socks into a ball.

"I know," Daddy says, winking, "how about a giraffe?"
"No." I shrug his arm off my shoulders.
"Right," Daddy says. "His neck would be far too long
to fit him into my shaving kit."
"Right?" Daddy asks, latching his suitcase.
"I don't want anything, Daddy," I answer as I run down
the hall to my room,
"from you," I whisper.

I GET into my pajamas and sit on my bed.
I hear Daddy's slow footsteps follow me into my room.

He sits down near me on the edge of my bed.
Moonlight falls over him like water
dripping in through my window.
All I can hear is the sound of my sister's breathing
from her crib across the room.
"I have to go," my daddy sighs.
His face is white as the moon itself, hanging over my bed.
His voice sounds crooked, too, when he clears his throat.
"I'll miss you so much," he says.
"More than you know," he whispers.

His hand is cold as he lays it on my cheek.

AND, just then, I know how bad he feels,
because I feel that way too.

"Each day that I am gone," Daddy says quietly,
"I will whisper your name to the wind
  as it sweeps across the sand,
  and ripples over the river,
  and jumps across the ocean
  to nestle, swirling, in the treetops outside your window."

"You would do that?" I ask him.
"Yes," he answers, "every day."

"Each night that I'm gone," he says,
"I will send you kisses, blown
  flying and diving out over the black sky
  like swooping night birds
  to settle with slender feet into your dreams."

"You would really do that?" I ask him.
"Yes," he answers, "every night."

"Each day that you're gone, Daddy," I tell him,
"I'll mark a big, red X on the calendar in the kitchen."
He nods.

"And each day that you're gone,
I will save up one thing for you.
To show you when you get back."
I reach into my hiding place under the bed.
"Like this," I tell him. I pull out my blue bottle cap.
"I found this flattened in the driveway."
I reach into my hiding place again.
"Like this," and I open my hand to show him my best
black rock. "I shined this up. It's my lucky rock,"
I tell him.

"You would do all that?" he asks me.
"Yes," I answer, "every day."

"And each night that you're gone," I tell my daddy,
"after Mom puts me to bed,
  whether I can see stars or the moon
  or dark white snowclouds out of my window,
  I will say, 'Good night, Daddy,' before I fall asleep."

"And you will wake each day with the wind from Africa
  and my kisses brushing your cheek,"
  Daddy whispers to me,
  as he tucks me in and sends me a kiss,
  blown from the doorway.

I close my eyes but I don't sleep.
Soon I hear a car honk outside.
When I go to my window,
I see Daddy get into a car with a light on top.
I watch as the light backs out of our driveway
and turns out into the street.
I watch until the light is gone.
"Good night, Daddy," I whisper,
and my breath makes a cloud
on the windowpane.

THE next day I find a gray bird feather
with a white dot at the tip.
"Daddy will like this," I tell my sister.
And I put it into the special box I found for Daddy,
right next to my special rock.

The day after that, I find a big pine cone
that rattles with seeds when I shake it.
"Daddy will like this," I tell my mom, and I put it
into my special box next to my bird feather.

Every day I find something more for Daddy:
a piece of green rope, a small lock without a key;
and I think of something new to tell him about
when he comes home.
And every night I say good night to him before I go to bed.

But every day feels longer than the one before
and every day my daddy feels further and further away.
So, I try to imagine Daddy in Africa
when I look at the map hanging on my bedroom wall.

AND when me and my mom fill our winter bird feeder
all the way to the top,
I try to imagine Daddy watching giant African birds
eating from giant African trees.
Mom tells me that big or small,
those African birds won't be shivering in the snow
like ours are.

Or when I follow the animal tracks
in the snow in our garden,
I try to imagine Daddy following lions in Africa,
over the rivers and across the sand.

But when it gets too cold for us to go outside at all,
we sit on the floor and play games and drink hot chocolate.
I look out our front window
and try to imagine Daddy sitting at his window, too,
looking out—

AND that's when I wonder if Daddy will ever come back at all.
So I listen really hard to see if I can hear him
whisper my name to the wind jumping over the river,
and I wait really quietly to see if I can feel his kisses,
blown from Africa into my dreams.

Uɴᴛɪʟ today.
Today is the day when I mark off the last X
on our calendar in the kitchen,
and I pull my special box from its hiding place
under my bed.

Today is the day that my mom and my sister
and me and my special box
get in a car with a light on the top and go to the airport—

WHERE I find carts with suitcases piled high,
and all kinds of people running, walking and talking,
but where I'm the one
who looks the hardest and the longest
through all of them.

AND I'm the one
who finds my daddy there,
back from Africa—
back with me.